It's an Ant's Life

If found, please return this journal to:

NAME   Ant

ADDRESS   Under the sidewalk by the red flowers

Personal details:

SIZE   Smaller than this dot ●.

OCCUPATION   Worker and forager (food collector)

HOBBIES   Work

COLORING   Almost black, like all my friends

FAVORITE FOOD   Honeydew (not the melon!) and other sugary things

FAVORITE WEATHER   Cool and damp

Reader's Digest Children's Books
are published by Reader's Digest Children's Publishing, Inc.
Reader's Digest Road, Pleasantville, NY 10570-7000
Visit our web site: www.readersdigestkids.com

Conceived, edited, and designed by Tucker Slingsby Limited
Berkeley House, 73 Upper Richmond Road, London SW15 2SZ

Illustrations by Tim Hayward, Robin Carter, and Adam Stower
Additional graphic manipulation by Adam Wilmot
Text by Steve Parker and Ant

Library of Congress Cataloging-in-Publication Data
Parker, Steve.
It's an Ant's Life / with the help of Steve Parker;
[illustrations by Tim Hayward, Robin Carter, and Adam Stower].
p. cm.
Summary: Presents all kinds of factual information about ants in
the form of a scrapbook prepared by one ant.
ISBN 1-57584-315-3
1. Ants—Juvenile literature. 2. Insect societies—Juvenile literature. [1. Ants.]
I. Hayward, Tim, ill. II. Carter, Robin, ill. III. Stower, Adam, ill. IV. Title.
QL568.F7P35 2000
595.79'6—dc21 99-11584

It's an Ant's Life

by Ant, with help from

Steve Parker

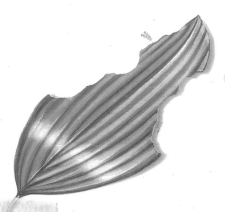

Reader's Digest Children's Books™
Pleasantville, New York * Montréal, Québec

MEET ME

I've got a few minutes to spare, so I can finally start my journal. Some of us have been given a short rest from work. But, like all ants, I like to stay busy, so I've only got time for a few facts about me and my friends.

All ants work very hard. We love it. Work is all we do and all we want to do. There's no time for playing. By the time I've worked, eaten, and rested, it's time to go back to work again. YIPPEE!

THIS WAS ME WHEN I WAS YOUNGER. I HAVEN'T CHANGED MUCH.

ME AND MY NESTMATES. WE ALL HAVE DIFFERENT JOBS TO DO. SOLDIERS GUARD OUR NEST, WORKERS KEEP THINGS NEAT AND CLEAN, AND FORAGERS LOOK FOR FOOD. WHEN I'M A BIT OLDER, I'M GOING TO BE A FORAGER!

LIST OF THINGS I KNOW

• Ants are tiny.

• Ants' brains are even tinier. We don't have much room for learning, but we are born knowing all we need to know—how to work.

• Ants are INSECTS.

I found all this out from "Old Ant," our oldest and wisest sister who knows EVERYTHING! Old Ant let me nibble some pages out of a book she found, which explains it all. I've taped some of the pages in my journal.

Rest period over—I'm on duty again. Back to work! HOORAY!

Insects of the World:

• There are over one million kinds of insects—more than all other animals added together.

• The biggest insects are moths and butterflies with 10-inch (25 cm) wingspans, stick insects 12 inches (30 cm) long, and goliath beetles weighing 3.5 ounces (100 g).

• Other kinds of insects are ants, bees, wasps, flies, grasshoppers, crickets, dragonflies, cockroaches, earwigs, lacewings, and fleas.

Grasshopper

← ME!

• A typical insect has six legs and three body parts—a head, a thorax, and an abdomen.

Moth

ME—BY ME

MY ANTENNAE (FEELERS)— FOR FEELING, SMELLING, TASTING, AND TAPPING

MY EYES— FOR SEEING

MY JAWS—FOR CUTTING UP FOOD AND HOLDING ONTO THINGS

MY ABDOMEN—MY FOOD GOES IN HERE AFTER I'VE EATEN IT

MY LEGS— FOR WALKING

THERE ARE MILLIONS AND MILLIONS OF ANTS IN THE WORLD—MORE ANTS THAN PEOPLE. WE MAY BE TINY, BUT I THINK WE'RE VERY IMPORTANT!

FRIENDS ON THE INTERNEST

All my nestmates look a lot like me. In fact, just like me. But I've got other ant friends, too. Here are some pictures they've sent me by snail mail and on the Internest. They live in nests far away from my sidewalk, and their lives sound very exciting! Like me, they are all busy, busy, busy.

SWEETS

My favorite pen pal! She's a honeypot ant from North America. She's sweet, gooey, and fat. Her abdomen is full of a sticky, sugary liquid. When her sisters stroke her, she oozes a bit of the liquid for them to drink. I bet it tastes great!

BITER

Look at those huge jaws! Biter's a bulldog ant—she lives in Australia. When her nest is attacked, Biter uses those jaws to bite her enemies. Sounds pretty useful to me!

Termite mounds on the African savanna

BIANCA

This postcard is from my friend Bianca who's not really an ant at all—she's a termite. You can see her nest on the left. It's very tall—much bigger than my nest. She lives there with millions of her sisters. The nest is in Africa, where it's very hot and dry. Bianca is very soft and white (not hard and black like me). But she's a sensible termite and spends most of her time in the dark, damp nest, away from the baking-hot sun.

JAWS

Jaws is a full-time soldier ant. She and her friends defend their nest from enemies who want to eat their eggs and grubs. Soldier ants have much bigger heads and jaws than I do. They're fierce!

LUCY

Lucy is called a leaf-cutter ant. She cuts off pieces of leaf with her jaws and carries them like a sunshade, and so do all her friends.

THAT'S LUCY

WHERE I LIVE

Another break, and a chance to write about our nest. It's big, with lots of tunnels and loads of chambers, or rooms . The roof is huge and hard and flat. Inside, it's just right— dark, cool, and damp! And it's very busy, with lots and lots of nestmates scurrying everywhere. Each of us learned our way around from a map we were given when we became adults.

I've never been outside. But I'm on the list to be a forager, so I should go out soon—CAN'T WAIT! Outside is where food comes from. Old Ant says it's even bigger than our nest. Some nestmates say the outside is dark, like the nest, but others say it's light and sunny. I guess I'll have to find out for myself.

BIG ROOT

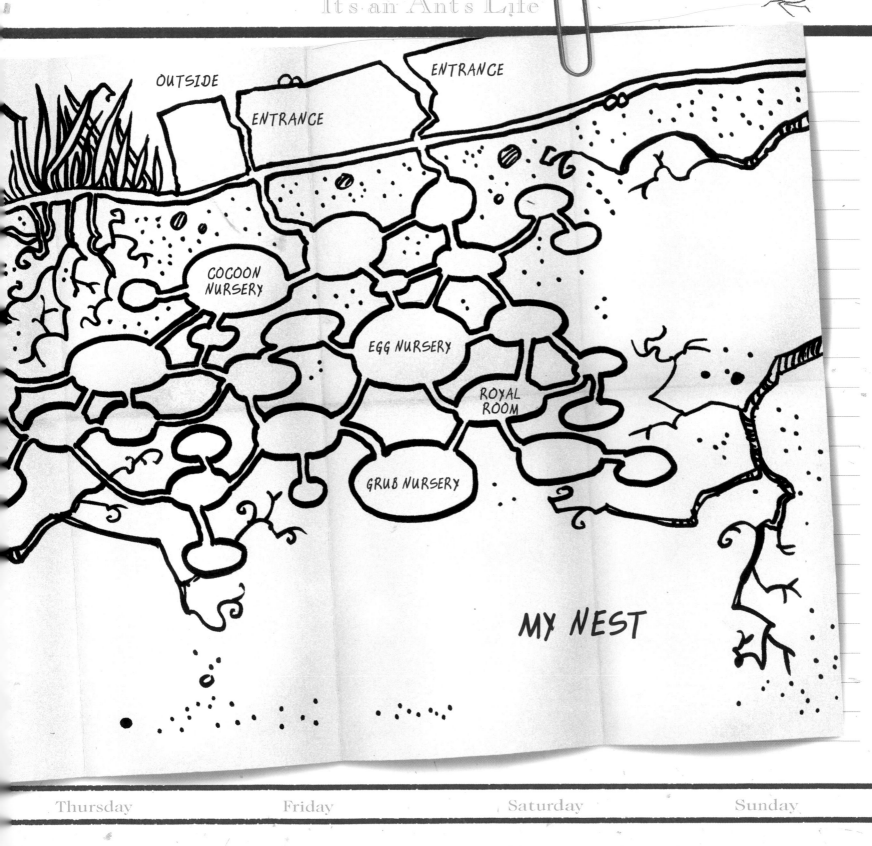

VISIT TO THE ROYAL CHAMBER

I've just seen the Queen! She's my mother. She's also mother to all of my nestmates. Our father died ages ago, even before Old Ant hatched—and she must be the oldest ant in the nest (apart from the Queen, of course!).

The Queen is ENORMOUS! She only has one job—laying eggs—and that keeps her busy. She lies in the royal chamber and lays dozens of eggs an hour. Today my job was to take the eggs to the Nursery. Last time, I was allowed to feed the Queen. Next time maybe I'll be allowed to clean away her droppings. What an honor!

WORK TO BE DONE
(BEFORE FIRST REST BREAK)

- Check eggs in Egg Nursery.
- Count grubs in Grub Nursery.
- See if cocoons in Cocoon Nursery have changed into grown-ups yet.

MY MOTHER, THE QUEEN (SHE'S IN THE MIDDLE)

GROWING UP

There are always babies of some kind in the nest. First eggs turn into grubs, then cocoons, and finally into ants, just like me. Old Ant says this is called "metamorphosis." Right now, my nestmates are all female. The Queen is our mother, so that makes us all sisters. Male ants appear later, at breeding time.

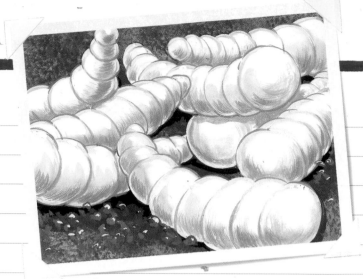

GREEDY GRUBS

Next I hatched into a grub, and then I was always hungry! Old Ant's book says another name for grub is "larva." Once the eggs in my group had all hatched, they renamed our room Grub Nursery 1A. We all wriggled, grew bigger, shed our skins (or molted), and ate all the time. The adult ants on nursery duty were always rushing around to keep us well fed.

EGG FIRST!

Today I was busy checking the nurseries, and it reminded me of my earliest days. I started off life as an egg in Egg Nursery 1A. I was small, round, and creamy white. Being an egg is kind of boring—you don't do anything.

SO MANY COCOONS BEING EATEN!

Food for the Fish
Give the fish in your pond a treat. Feed them ant eggs. They are nutritious and can be dug up in your garden.

← THESE ARE COCOONS—NOT EGGS!

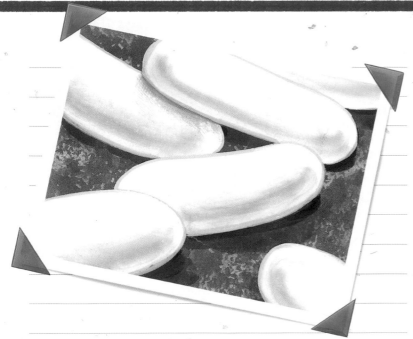

DRAWINGS—BY ME

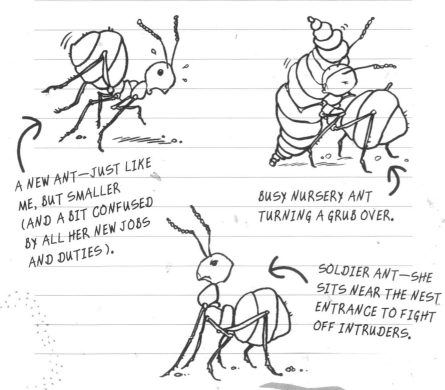

A NEW ANT—JUST LIKE ME, BUT SMALLER (AND A BIT CONFUSED BY ALL HER NEW JOBS AND DUTIES).

BUSY NURSERY ANT TURNING A GRUB OVER.

SOLDIER ANT—SHE SITS NEAR THE NEST ENTRANCE TO FIGHT OFF INTRUDERS.

COZY, LAZY COCOONS

I can remember feeling completely exhausted after all that eating. All of us grubs then turned into cocoons. I can't remember much about that stage. I think I just rested— without eating any more food. Old Ant says that cocoons are also called "pupae."

THE BIG DAY

This picture shows me just minutes after breaking out of my cocoon! At last I was a grown-up ant. I was handed a map of the nest and a list of jobs and duties. I felt VERY important.

ANOTHER BUSY, BUSY DAY

Today, I've been working in the nursery. I had so many jobs! Here's what I did . . .

• I fanned some eggs by waving my antennae and legs to keep them cool. The nest is very warm now. It seems to get warm, then cool, then warm again, and so on. Old Ant says it's called "day" and "night," whatever that means.

• I cleaned, rolled, and turned some eggs to make sure they don't get moldy and die.

• I moved some eggs from one chamber to another. A group of workers is going to make the old chamber bigger because our nest is getting too crowded.

FEEDING GRUBS

• I cleared away molted skins. Grubs shed their skins a lot as they grow, especially when they turn into cocoons.

• I cleaned up some grubby grubs and carried away their droppings.

• I fed some grubs. They eat a sticky soup made from all kinds of things. We mix together leaf sap, nectar from flowers, seeds, and chewed-up worms. Yummy! The grubs grow very quickly on this tasty diet.

CLEARING AWAY DROPPINGS

NURSERY DUTY

Fan, clean, and turn eggs
Mix food and chew up worms for grubs
Scrub grubs
Clear out droppings, molted skins, dead grubs, and broken body parts

TURNING EGGS

EGG FANNING

EGG MOVING

ME AND MY FELLOW WORKERS ON
NURSERY DUTY. LOOK HOW BUSY WE ARE!
I THINK WE KEEP THE CLEANEST, NEATEST
NURSERY IN THE **WHOLE** WORLD!

CLEANING UP MOLTED SKINS

MIXING FOOD

GRUB-SCRUBBING

Thursday   Friday   Saturday   Sunday

TALL RED BLOCKS STACKED UP TO THE SKY

OUTSIDE AT LAST!

Wow! Today I followed a forager and we went outside! First, she tapped the ground with her antennae to pick up the trail. This is a scent trail that earlier foragers put down as they go along. Old Ant calls the scent "pheromone." If we follow the scent trail, it will lead us straight to the food, and we won't get lost.

These early foragers must be very BRAVE to go out and look for food. It's a jungle out there! The green strips—called grass—are so tall, I can't see their tops. There are huge green flat things that take forever to walk across. They're called leaves.

Outside was light and bright. I'm told it'll get dark later on. Weird, huh? So that's what day and night are all about!

ENEMY ATTACK!

Today was SO SCARY, I can hardly write! Ladybug came too close to our nest. I'm sure she wanted to eat us or carry away our grubs and cocoons. Hundreds of my sisters and I all tapped our antennae and gave off our alarm scent. "ATTACK THE ENEMY!" it said.

One group of soldiers stood right in front of Ladybug. They tried to bite her. But she was biting back, too. She even chomped one ant in half! Soldiers squirted something nasty called acid at Ladybug. They aimed their backsides at her and fired the acid where it would hurt—at Ladybug's eyes and antennae. It seemed to really sting her.

But she still didn't go! So more soldiers ran behind her. They bit her legs and backside, and squirted more acid. Ladybug finally realized our nest was too big and there were too many of us. She gave up and crawled away. But I bet she'll be back.

Giant Anteater

This long-nosed, long-tailed, long-haired mammal has a body 3 feet (1 m) long. It lives in Central and South America. The giant anteater can rip open even the thickest ant-nest walls with its huge front claws. It eats about 10,000 ants each day, licking them up with its long, sticky tongue. But it only takes a few hundred ants from each nest, then moves to another, leaving some ants to repair the nests so they're ready to yield more food a week or two later.

IT'S ENORMOUS!

After the battle, we were exhausted. Some of the older soldiers told me about other enemies, and I drew pictures of some of them. I also found a picture of a terrifying, enormous ant-killer in Old Ant's book!

ANT ENEMY NUMBER 3 : "BEETLE"

ANT ENEMY NUMBER 12 : "WASP"

SPILLS AND THRILLS

Another exciting day! I went outside again because the early foragers had found a new source of food. Old Ant says it's called a picnic. There were all kinds of yummy things spread out on the grass. I'd never seen or tasted most of them before.

We sent signals back to the nest—"We need more foragers!" Soon there were lots of us, scuttling around and snipping off pieces of food to carry back to the nest.

Some of the foods were awful. The giant green and red thing covering the grass was fuzzy and tasteless. The shiny silver things were too hard to bite and very slippery to walk on. But other foods were delicious, like the hard white lumps. They tasted sweet—like the nectar we get from flowers.

New Foods I Tried Today

I described the food to Old Ant. She told me what they were so I could write them down:

• The sweet white lumps are called sugar.

• Strawberries—huge red balls with seeds on them. Taste sweet and juicy.

• Bread—a giant white slab with small, spongy holes in it. It tastes slightly sweet, sort of like grass seeds.

• Pink, flaky stuff on the bread. Tastes salty. Old Ant thinks it's salmon, a big fish. (Whatever that is!)

• Jam-filled cake—DELICIOUS! Sweet, gooey stuff inside two moist, crumbly layers.

• Huge, greenish tube, hard and slippery. Tastes sour. It's called a pickle. Yucky!

I BROUGHT THIS BLOB OF FRUITY JAM BACK, BUT IT STUCK TO THE PAGE. WHEN NO ONE'S LOOKING, I'LL JUST NIBBLE IT UP!

GUESTS IN THE NEST

I have been very busy today, taking a survey of the nest. The Queen asked me to list all the not-ants living with us at the moment. There are always lodgers and visitors down here. They like dark and cool places, too.

It's a good thing that I've got sensitive antennae. Otherwise, I couldn't tap my nestmates to talk to them. My antennae also help me feel my way around and find the not-ants in the dark.

Some not-ants are heaps of trouble! One of the worst is Spider—she's big and she moves in a sneaky, silent way. Sometimes she steals our eggs and cocoons, so we're always on the lookout for her. She's even older than Old Ant!

Some not-ants, like Woodlouse, are no trouble. She eats old, empty cocoons, molted skins from our grubs, empty ants' eggshells, and even grub droppings. We have to pick up droppings when we're cleaning, but we'd never eat them. Yuck! In general, she helps to keep the nest clean and neat. I sometimes tap her with my antennae to say "thank you."

Our most favorite not-ants are Aphids. But they live outside on a farm. I hope to visit them tomorrow.

HONEYDEW—YUM! YUM!
(It's not very easy to draw)

ON THE FARM

Today I went outside with the farmer ants. We marched to a big plant covered with strange creatures called aphids. They have six legs like me but they're smaller, hairier, and some are BRIGHT GREEN!

When you stroke an aphid, it oozes a sweet, sticky juice from its backside! We call it "honeydew." It tastes delicious!

MY FAVORITE APHID

Ants get along well with aphids. They eat plants and make honeydew. We eat the honeydew and in return we protect the aphids from fierce aphid-eaters, like Ladybug. An ant can get killed that way! I think being a farmer ant is the most DANGEROUS job in the whole nest. Luckily, I don't have to do it very often!

Looking after aphids is hard work. Sometimes farmer ants have to move them to a safer place. And it can take FOREVER! Aphids are so slow and stupid. Not like us—we are quick, clever, AND we do what we're told!

It was a long, scary day, but we all made it back to the nest, safe and sound. After we got home, we spit up some of the honeydew we'd eaten and shared it with our nestmates. WHAT A PARTY!

ANTS EAT MOLDY LEAVES!

Fungus, or leaf-cutter, ants in North America live in gigantic nests in vast underground caves. The ants cut up leaves and bring them back to the nest. There they chew them up and dampen them with spit and droppings. After a while, the leaf pieces grow moldy and the ants eat the fungus.

SO THAT'S WHAT LUCY DOES WITH THOSE LEAVES!

SWARM IN THE WARM

Today was STRANGE! The weather's been so muggy lately, and the nest has been so crowded that we've all been on edge. Suddenly, lots of my nestmates left home, just like that.

I was watching the latest batch of grown-ups come out of their cocoons. There were sisters—and to my amazement, BROTHERS, TOO! The first male ants I've ever seen! Each new ant had four thin and flappy body parts. Old Ant called these things "wings."

First they stood at the nest entrances, then they flapped their wings and suddenly rose into the air. They were F-ANT-ASTIC! Old Ant says they will fly until they meet winged ants from other nests. Then they will mate and breed. The male ants will die, but the females will become queen ants and set up new nests far away.

FLYING ANTS EVERYWHERE! THEY'RE EVEN SMALLER THAN I AM!

THIS WING FELL OFF ONE OF MY NESTMATES. BET HE DIDN'T FLY FAR!

Thursday   Friday   Saturday   Sunday

THE GREAT DISASTER!

This is the first rest break I've had all day. Disaster struck the nest, and we all had to work really hard without stopping. Whew!

Just after the winged ants left, there was a huge storm. Usually, when it rains, a bit of water trickles into our nest. Sister nestworkers soon fix any damage. But this time, the water just POURED in. Water gushed through the tunnels and flooded the chambers. It was terrible—eggs, grubs, and cocoons got SWEPT away. The nursery walls turned to mud and the ceilings fell in. Lots of foragers and nursery workers were trapped and couldn't get out. It was an awful mess!

But we ants are not easily beaten. We worked hard to rescue all the eggs, grubs, and cocoons we could, and started to repair the damage. By tomorrow, I bet the nest will be almost as good as new.

EMERGENCY

Volunteers needed in all areas.
We must all work harder than ever to
make the nest fit for our Queen again.

YOUR NEST NEEDS YOU!

DAMAGE REPORT

Entrances	seven blocked
Tunnels	nineteen collapsed
Tunnels	two filled with soil
Tunnels	one filled with stones
Chambers	ten caved in

BRAVERY AWARDS

To be awarded to 9 nursery workers for
helping our Queen through the escape
tunnel and saving her life.

SUN AGAIN

Yesterday was a very bad day. But now the sun's come out again, and all the survivors are back doing their old jobs.

Old Ant slipped in a wet tunnel yesterday and hurt her leg. Well, she is very old and doesn't move as quickly as she used to. It happens to the best of us ants. We start walking instead of running everywhere. Then we need more and more rest breaks and start making mistakes. I think that Old Ant will soon have to stop working.

When it happens, some of the others will look after her. Like all ants, Old Ant has always loved working, so she'll probably miss it when she retires. Luckily, I still have lots of time to work before I have to retire. Collecting nectar from the flowers is today's job.

The days are getting shorter and I think the dark, cold time that Old Ant warned us about will soon be here. She called it "winter." It's time to put this journal away carefully. Perhaps next year another ant will continue my story. It's been quite a time what with the ladybug attack, the strange winged ants leaving home, and the great flood. I wonder if next year will be as interesting.

MY FAVORITE FLOWERS— CAREFULLY PRESSED BY ME

Geranium petal

Rose petal

Violet

Honeysuckle

OLD ANT'S WISE WORDS

Old Ant has a great memory. She knows more than 10 things! I wrote them down
so that we'll know them, too, even after she's gone.

ABDOMEN
The rear part of an ant's body, behind the part with the legs. An ant's body is divided into three parts—the head, the thorax, and the abdomen.

EGG
The first stage of an ant's life. Eggs are laid by the Queen.

GRUB
The second stage of an ant's life, after the egg, but before the cocoon. Also called the larva (plural: larvae).

HEAD
The front part of an ant's body, with the mouth, jaws, eyes, and antennae.

HONEYDEW
A sweet, sticky liquid that aphids and similar creatures ooze from their backsides. Ants drink it.

NECTAR
A sweet, sticky liquid that flowers make. We ants and other insects, such as bees and wasps, love it!

ADULT
The last and busiest stage of an ant's life. A grown-up, with six legs—not an egg, grub, or cocoon.

ANTENNAE
Feelers—two long thin parts on the head that are used for touching, smelling, tasting, tapping, and talking.

COCOON
The third stage of an ant's life, after the grub, but before the adult. Also called the pupa (plural: pupae).

LARVA
A fancy name for a grub.

METAMORPHOSIS
The way some creatures change as they grow up. I did—from egg to grub, to cocoon, to adult. So did Moth, who was once a caterpillar.

PHEROMONES
Trails or signals that ants can't see, but that we can smell or detect. Different pheromones tell ants to do certain things, like forage for food, repair the nest or attack invading enemies.

PUPA
A fancy name for a cocoon (plural: pupae).

THORAX
The middle part of an ant's body, including the legs (and in some ants, the wings, too).